ILLUMINATION PRESENTS

THE SECRET LIFE OF Pets 2

MAX ON THE FARM!

Adapted by David Lewman
Illustrated by Elsa Chang

A GOLDEN BOOK • NEW YORK

© 2019 Universal Studios. The Secret Life of Pets 2 is a trademark and copyright of Universal Studios.
All Rights Reserved. Published in the United States by Golden Books, an imprint of Random House
Children's Books, a division of Penguin Random House LLC, 1745 Broadway, New York, NY 10019,
and in Canada by Penguin Random House Canada Limited, Toronto. Golden Books, A Golden Book,
A Little Golden Book, the G colophon, and the distinctive gold spine are registered trademarks
of Penguin Random House LLC.
rhcbooks.com
Educators and librarians, for a variety of teaching tools,
visit us at RHTeachersLibrarians.com
ISBN 978-1-9848-4994-6 (trade) — ISBN 978-1-9848-4995-3 (ebook)
Printed in the United States of America
10 9 8 7 6 5 4 3 2

Max was a city dog. He loved living in New York!
But worrying about baby Liam going to preschool
made Max nervous. He started scratching too much!
   His owners, Katie and Chuck, thought that some
fresh air might do everyone some good. They
took Max, Duke, and even baby Liam to visit
Uncle Shep's farm.

Duke loved it! But Max thought
everything he ran into was scary:

a big spider ...

a bunch of unfriendly cows ...

a noisy tractor . . .

VROOM VROOM

and a mean turkey!

GOBBLE GOBBLE!

"I am not a fan of the farm," Max said.

From his special spot on an old truck, the big farm dog, Rooster, watched the turkey chase the scared little city dog. He let out one loud *WOOF,* and the turkey stopped chasing Max.

WOOF!

That night, Max and Duke had to sleep outside.
Duke slept soundly, but Max was nervous about
all the strange sounds coming from the farm.

SQUAWK

CHEEP

GROWL

GRUNT

HOO HOO

CROAK

ZZZZ

SNORT GOBBLE

Max tried to find a quiet spot, but he ended up being chased by a fox! Luckily, Rooster chased the fox away. Max wished he was as brave as Rooster.

The next morning, Max and Duke watched Rooster
stop a cattle stampede. "So cool!" Duke said.

Later, Max and Duke saw a pig escape from
the barn. Duke thought they should tell Rooster.
But Max said he could handle it.

SQUEAL!

"Hey, mister!" Max yelled. "Back inside!"
But the pig ignored Max, even when the
little dog jumped onto the pig's back.
Finally, Max bit the pig's tail. The pig
squealed and sent Max flying!

Then the sheep escaped from their pen through the gap Max had made. Rooster ran up and herded them back in, but a sheep named Cotton was missing.

Rooster made Max go with him to look for the lost sheep in the dark, scary woods. Max thought Duke should come, too, but Rooster said, "Just you and me."

In the woods, Max had trouble keeping up with Rooster.

He fell into the water ...

got stuck in sticker-bushes ...

fell down a hill . . .

and almost stepped on a snake!

Finally, they found Cotton stuck in a tree wedged in the side of a cliff. "That tree won't hold my weight," Rooster said. He called to Cotton, "Max is coming down to save you!" Max was terrified!

Rooster taught Max a trick. "The first step of
not being afraid," he explained, "is acting like
you're not afraid." Max slowly climbed down to
Cotton. But the tree slipped and started to fall!

THUMP! The tree caught on the other side of the ravine. Max reached Cotton and swung him up onto a ledge.

Then Max pushed Cotton up the cliff to the top. But Max lost his grip and started to fall! *"AHHHHH!"* he screamed.

Rooster caught Max's collar in his mouth and yanked him up. He was safe! And so was Cotton! When they returned the missing sheep to the farm, Max felt SO PROUD! He felt like a completely different dog.

"Hey, kid. Good job today," Rooster said to Max.

That night, Rooster invited
Max up onto the truck to join
him in a good, long *HOWL!*

Later, when Max was asleep, Rooster
gave him a present: a really cool bandanna,
just like the one Rooster wore!

The next morning, Max and Duke went back to the city.

"Bye, Rooster!" Duke said.

"And thanks!" Max called.

Max had been scared about everything when he first got on the farm, but now he felt like he could do anything.